I0624772

THE VAMPIRE'S OMEN

SHAWN WISEMAN

TABLE OF CONTENTS

PROLOGUE

Detective Simmons sat in his car, the ceiling light illuminating the interior as he took drags from his cigarette. The smoke filtered into the vehicle despite his attempts to blow it out the window. The keys were in the ignition, but the car was not running. Simmons was waiting for someone.

Simmons stared into the darkness of the alley he was parked in, his eyes moving from shadow to shadow as he waited for someone to appear. There was a pain in his shoulder and he moved his free hand to rub the wound there. Though it was no longer bleeding and didn't need bandages, there were two marks from a vampire bite that had hit clean down to the nerves. He could touch the wound and not feel it, but the pain was still there in the surrounding tissue. He would have a scar there the rest of his life, he imagined. A constant reminder of his failure, and of the freak hybrid who gave it to him.

After he rolled his shoulder and went back to staring at shadows, he noticed movement in the back seat of his car. There was a man sitting there, shrouded in shadows and a hood.

"Jesus fuck, can you not do that?" Simmons shouted.

"Perhaps if you paid a bit more attention to your surroundings, you would not have been startled," the man replied.

"Yeah, well, right now I have two pains in the neck. This…" Simmons said, pointing to where he was bitten, "and you. I can't pay attention to both at the same time."

"The boss is displeased," the man hissed, ignoring Simmons' comment.

"Tch," Simmons scoffed. "*I'm* displeased. You think I wanted it to go down the way it did? How was I supposed to know they had some freak of nature on their side? I didn't even know there was such a thing as a vampire psychic."

"Failure is not tolerated… but the boss understands the… unique challenges which presented themselves. We were also surprised by the development, so the boss is giving you a second chance to make things right."

Simmons' eyes widened. "Yeah?"

"Yes," the man replied, devoid of expression and tone.

"I guarantee this time it's going to be different. I have just the person for the job. A real professional scumbag."

"There is one change, however. The target is different. The boss thinks we cast too wide a net, so begin by finishing the job you started first. Kill the one you stole your trophy from."

Simmons chuckled. "You got it, chief. This'll be a piece of cake. I already have her address."

"Don't fail us this time," he warned.

"Right," Simmons replied before pursing his lips. The man started to leave the detective's car, but the detective stopped him. "Hey, wait just a minute. I got a question. Why didn't I turn into a vampire after I got bit? Can you explain that to me?"

"Unlike popular fiction, vampirism is not a virus or affliction. It is genetics, just as your powers are. We are all descendant from humans."

"Huh," the detective muttered. "Makes you wonder why we're at odds with each other, doesn't it?"

The other man left the vehicle. "Yes," he agreed. "Yes it does."

1. AN ILL OMEN

"How's the popcorn coming?" Olivia yelled from her couch.

"It's just started popping now," Kara replied from the kitchen.

She was standing over a hot stove with corn kernels sitting in a pot of oil. The kernels started doing their dance and opening up, releasing a fragrant smell into the air. Kara shook the pot to keep the popped kernels from burning, and soon the pot was filled to the brim with fresh popcorn. She placed them in a bowl and threw some salt on top to add flavour, then went to Olivia's living room and sat down on the couch.

Olivia also looked ready to burst with anticipation. "Popcorn!" she yelled as she threw her arms in the air.

Kara laughed at her friend's enthusiasm. She took a handful of the popcorn and then handed the bowl to Olivia. "You're always so excited when it comes to food."

Olivia stuffed her face with a handful of popcorn, and after chomping down on it a bit she was able to talk. "That's why we make such a great team. You like to cook, I like to eat."

Kara pouted. "And yet you somehow manage to stay slim. I'm jealous."

"Well, that's what training for four hours a day will do for you. You have a great figure too. You just hide it behind hoodies and sweaters all the time." Olivia pointed at Kara's baggy blue hoodie. "If you want to you can join me."

Kara shook her head. "No thank you. I'm fine with being lazy. Besides, I thought you used to only do two hours a day. That would be much more manageable. Not that I'd do that either," she added in a whisper.

"It used to be two hours, but I increased it."

"Why?" Kara asked, but she immediately thought of why.

Olivia glanced her way. "Yeah. We weren't strong enough to take on one psychic, and we nearly died because of it. We were lucky there was someone else there to help us, but we can't rely on luck all the time. That's why it's four hours now."

Silence invaded the room as Kara thought on her selfishness and her weakness. Her weakness almost cost not only her life, but Olivia's life as well. *Maybe I should start training.*

Olivia coughed to break the silence. "I'm surprised Raymond's late, he's always on time," she said while taking another fistful of popcorn.

"He should be here soon. He texted me before I started making the popcorn."

"It's nice that we're all hanging out together again," Olivia said with a smile. "Well, most of us."

Kara knew she was talking about Damien, her ex. Before she could dwell too long on his betrayal, Olivia brought her back to here and now.

"Fuck him," she said.

Kara looked at her friend and smiled. "Fuck him," she repeated.

There was a knock at the door. "That must be Raymond," Olivia said, not moving.

Kara raised her brow and stared at Olivia. "Aren't you going to get the door? This is your apartment."

Olivia had a serious look on her face. "I have to guard the popcorn."

Kara burst out laughing, and then she got up from the couch. She shook her head as she went to the door. "No one's going to steal it. We're the only ones here."

"You don't know that," she replied with her brows furrowed.

Kara opened the door, and Raymond was standing there with a bottle of wine in one hand and chips in the other. "Hey Ray, come in."

"You're late," Olivia shouted from the couch, still guarding the popcorn.

Raymond pushed his glasses up on his nose. "Sorry, I thought I would bring some wine and snacks."

"Ray! You're here! Come in, come in. Sit beside me," Olivia said, with a smile this time.

"At least we know how to make Olivia happy," Ray commented.

The Vampire's Omen

"Isn't that the truth?" Kara closed the door and went back to her place on the sofa.

Raymond removed his shoes and coat, and then placed the wine and chips on her coffee table. He went to her kitchen and got some wine glasses for everyone. "Did you have your surgery yet, Olivia?" he asked.

"No, not yet. Still have these damn dentures in. I scheduled it for next week, and then I won't have to worry about this anymore. That is until I—"

"Until you find that detective who took your fang from you," Kara interrupted. "We know all about it, Liv. You're sounding like a broken record at this point."

"I'll show you a broken record," Olivia mumbled. "I'll break *his* record."

Kara shook her head and accepted a wine glass from Raymond. "So, what do you guys want to watch?"

"As long as it's not an action movie I'm fine with anything," Olivia said.

Raymond and Kara both groaned. "You of all people should love action movies, Liv. I can't understand it."

"They're unrealistic. I can't get past how foolish the fights are."

"How about we watch that new thriller that just came out. I can't remember the name." Raymond held his hand to his chin as he tried to think of the movie.

"I think I know the one you're talking about," Olivia said with a nod. "I'm fine with watching that."

After pouring the wine and opening the bags of chips, they put on a video streaming service and began watching the movie. It was full of suspense and had enough action that Raymond and Kara were both enjoying it, but not so much that Olivia couldn't get into it as well.

About halfway through the movie, Kara felt something in the back of her mind. She tensed as a feeling of dread washed over her. At first she thought it was the movie, but after a few seconds she recognized the feeling for what it was. She was sensing someone's approaching death. She took in a deep breath and closed her eyes. The only way to get rid of the feeling was to let it pass.

When she closed her eyes, the vision took over, and what she saw confused her even more. She could see Olivia's apartment, and lying back on the couch was Olivia, a dark red bloodstain around her head on both sides. It looked like she had been shot in the head.

Kara suppressed a scream and opened her eyes. The foreboding was growing stronger, and she knew that if she didn't act now then Olivia was gone.

Kara thrust her hand out towards the balcony window and focused her mental powers in that direction. In an instant she put up a barrier of psychic energy between her and the window. She made the air thick with the invisible force.

Before they heard the sound of the rifle, the bullet hurtled through the window. It broke the glass with a small crack, and hit Kara's barrier. The bullet was too fast and too strong, and it pushed its way through. She could feel it moving through the barrier like it was ripping through her mind. She pushed back with an equal force, straining her mind and body to pour more energy into stopping the speeding bullet. She clenched her teeth and fists, curled her toes, and furrowed her brows. She could feel the bullet slowing. It felt like it was pushing her whole body back, but she stood her ground. Every inch it moved was like a dagger stabbing her entire body. The bullet slowed and slowed until it came to a stop two inches in front of Olivia's face.

The time that passed was a mere fraction of a second, but to Kara it had felt like an eternity. She let out the breath she had been holding and collapsed on the floor. The bullet fell to the floor along with her, and her friends rushed to her aid.

"Kara!" they shouted, not understanding what had just happened.

Kara was convulsing on the floor, her nose and ears bleeding.

Olivia and Raymond were in total panic and didn't know what to do to help Kara. Before they could gather their wits, something blew the balcony doors off their hinges, and the glass shattered. Thousands of glass shards darted from the balcony and sliced the walls, the furniture, and the tiles of the floor. Olivia and Raymond ducked down and covered Kara with their bodies. The coffee table protected them from the glass. On the balcony, a man in black combat gear appeared with a mask shrouding his face. He held a curved knife in front of him as he walked inside the apartment.

Olivia gritted her teeth and ran over to the man. She went to punch him in the face, but he sidestepped out of the way. He put his free hand on the back of her neck and used her momentum to control her movement. He raised the curved knife in the air, and brought it back down in one motion, aiming for the back of Olivia's neck.

Raymond tackled the man to the ground, grabbing onto the hand with the knife. With a tight squeeze on his wrist, the man involuntarily let go of the knife. Raymond's eyes focussed squarely on the man's neck. He snarled, baring his fangs, and lunged forward to take a bite out of the man's larynx. An invisible force stopped him, and then threw him towards the wall.

Olivia was back on her feet and leapt into the air towards their psychic attacker. She slammed her fist down. He rolled out of the way, grabbing his knife as he did so. Olivia's fist left an indent in the marble tile.

The attacker raised the knife to eye level and stared down Olivia. Raymond rose to his feet and went behind the psychic. The two vampires stepped towards the psychic slowly, not attacking, but not backing down.

The psychic sent a blast of energy towards Raymond, but he was able to dodge out of the way, and it only hit him on the shoulder. The psychic used his gained time to move forward and attack Olivia. He slashed at her with the knife again and again, but she was able to dodge out the way.

Olivia grabbed his arms and held him. Raymond appeared behind him and helped Olivia wrap his arms around his back. The whole time, he was struggling with his psychic powers to push against the brute strength of the vampires. After Raymond had a firm grasp on the man's hands, Olivia released him and went to stab him in the stomach with her razor-sharp nails.

The man twisted his body and pushed Olivia's hand away. He jumped, kicked off the couch, and flipped over Raymond. Raymond couldn't keep his grip and let go of the assassin.

Kara flopped onto the bed, blood streaming from her nose and ears. She held her hand out and used what little strength she had to bind the psychic with her own powers. "Now!" she yelled as forcefully as she could.

Olivia and Raymond both glanced back at her, shocked she was still conscious, and then turned back to the psychic.

Kara held the psychic in place, and his eyes widened. Olivia and Raymond both rushed towards him, their claws poised to slash his neck and stomach. Just as they were about to make contact, he broke free from Kara's force and was able to move. Olivia managed to slash the side of his stomach before he got out of the way.

The assassin ran and jumped out the shattered windows as he clutched his side. Olivia and Raymond darted to the balcony only to see the psychic assassin floating to the ground and jumping into a vehicle. Olivia might have given chase if there weren't more important things she had to worry about.

Olivia and Raymond ran back over to the couch to see Kara lying down on it, wincing in pain. She was going in and out of consciousness, and from what they could tell she was still bleeding.

"We can't stay here," Raymond said. "There could be more people coming."

"Where can we go? We need to get Kara medical attention."

"For now, we should head to my place."

Olivia picked up Kara in her arms. "Let's go," she commanded.

They left the apartment, watching every shadow as they headed to Raymond's vehicle. Along the way, they saw the broken glass which had fallen from Olivia's balcony, and the blood of the man who'd tried to assassinate them.

"He'll pay for what he did to you, Kara," Olivia whispered. "I swear it."

2. PLASMA POTION

Olivia and Raymond busted through the door of his house. They went into the living room and gently placed Kara on the couch.

"Can you get me a wet cloth, Raymond?"

Raymond nodded and went into the kitchen. Olivia held her hand against Kara's forehead; she was running a fever. Her breathing came in ragged spurts. Olivia propped up a pillow and laid Kara down and made her as comfortable as possible.

Raymond returned with a warm, wet cloth and handed it to Olivia. She used it to clean Kara's nose and ears. She didn't seem to be bleeding anymore, but the bullet had taken its toll already.

"When did the doc say he would arrive?"

"In a half hour."

"I hope she'll be alright until then."

Olivia gave Raymond a stern look. "She will."

Raymond nodded, and then watched Kara. She was sweating and twitched back and forth like she was having a bad dream.

The sound of footsteps met their ears, and Damien came into the living room. He glanced around the room at the two open sets of eyes meeting him, and the one closed set.

"What happened?" he asked. His tone of voice and the look in his eyes showed sincere concern.

Olivia stared daggers at Damien. "None of your business."

Damien pursed his lips and cast his look away, like he wanted to say something, but shame stopped him. He took a breath and looked at Kara again, then at Olivia. "I'm just concerned, alright? Please just tell me what happened."

Olivia let out a sigh. "As far as I can tell, someone tried to kill us. They used a sniper rifle first, but Kara stopped the bullet in midair with her powers. It looks like she strained herself too far to stop it, and now she's unconscious."

Damien looked distressed. "Jesus. I didn't even know that was possible." He sat down on a coffee table in front of the couch.

"Neither did I. She nearly killed herself, so I don't think many psychics would try the same thing."

Damien was speechless. Olivia looked into his eyes, and she could tell that despite all he'd done and the hate he felt, he was concerned for Kara.

They waited in silence for the doctor to arrive, and after a half hour, right at the time he said he would arrive, there was a knock at the door.

Raymond let the doctor in and showed him over to Kara. The doctor nodded to Damien and Olivia as they moved out of the way for him to examine Kara.

He started by feeling her forehead, then he opened her mouth and used a small flashlight to look inside, and then he did the same with her eyes.

"How long has she been unconscious?" he asked.

"For about an hour now," Olivia replied.

"Hmm." The doctor continued his examination by checking her arms and legs, and then started getting out something from a bag he'd brought with him. "How did this happen?"

Olivia and Raymond glanced at each other. They were unsure how to broach the subject. The doctor was a vampire.

Damien growled. "She's the half-breed. She strained herself while using her powers and fell unconscious."

Olivia and Raymond were in shock from Damien's statement, but couldn't think of a rebuttal to the truth. The doctor's eyes went wide as his gaze went from Damien to the others in the room and then over to Kara. He began packing his things back up. "I'm sorry, I..."

Damien stood up and crossed his arms. He directed a menacing stare at the doctor that would have intimidated any person, vampire or no. "You'll do your job, that's what you were about to say, weren't you?"

The doctor began to sweat and turned back around and removed his tools again. He took out a stethoscope and checked various parts of her body. After a few moments he finished his examination.

The Vampire's Omen

"Truthfully, without further testing I cannot tell you what is wrong with her. I don't know enough about... their physiology to make a deduction."

"Then can you at least give us your best guess?"

"Well, the brain is like a muscle, so if she was doing something strenuous, it could be that she simply needs to rest. As she is like us, ingesting some blood might speed up recovery."

"And that's your professional opinion?" Damien questioned.

"Yes," the doctor replied. "May I go now? There's nothing more that I can do."

Damien moved aside, allowing the doctor room to leave. After he was out of the apartment, Damien started to leave the living room.

"Where are you going?" Olivia asked.

"To get some blood," he replied.

"Don't bother." Olivia got up and went over to Damien.

Damien stopped and turned around. "Why not?"

"Kara won't drink the blood of the living, so anything you have is no good."

Damien furrowed his brows, his porcelain skin wrinkling in anger. "This isn't the time for that nonsense. If someone's after you guys you need to be mobile, and the faster Kara recovers the faster you can find this guy and stop him."

Olivia bared her fang at Damien in equal fury. "So you're saying that her beliefs and her choice don't matter? You're just going to shove that blood down her throat when she can't even make the decision for herself? You make me sick," Olivia spat.

"Where are you going to find someone to get your blood from then? Tell me that!" Damien shouted. "Where are you going to find a recently deceased person to draw blood from? Her convictions aren't worth shit if she's dead."

Olivia looked like she'd been struck across the face, and she retaliated as such. She reared back and went to punch Damien in the stomach. He grabbed her arm to stop her.

Olivia wrenched her arm away, and then went back over to Kara. She picked her up in her arms. "C'mon Raymond, I don't trust leaving Kara here."

Raymond followed Olivia without question, and they left the apartment. They placed Kara in the back seat of Raymond's car before getting in the front themselves.

"So, what are we going to do?"

Olivia let out an angry sigh and leaned back in the car seat. "I don't know." She sat there with her eyes closed for a moment. "If we give Kara blood we took from the living she'll never forgive us, but right now we're sitting ducks dragging her around. If only Kara had some blood on her."

"You checked her pockets?" Raymond asked.

"Yeah, I just checked when I put her in the car."

"Well, what about her home? She must have a stash there, even if it's for emergencies."

Olivia opened her eyes and sat up straight. "You might be right. Let's go there first, and we can worry later if we don't find anything."

Raymond drove to Kara's, and parked on the side of the street next to the brick building.

"Alright, you stay here and I'll search for the blood."

Raymond raised his brow. "Wouldn't it be better if we both searched and brought Kara with us?"

"I don't want to deal with questions from her roommate."

"She has a roommate?" Raymond asked.

"Yeah, an old human."

"A human?"

Olivia laughed. "She met him after seeing his death in a vision, but it never came true, no matter how many times she felt it. She somehow ended up becoming his caretaker after that."

Raymond looked at Kara and smiled. "That seems like something she would do."

Olivia chuckled. "Yeah, it does." For another moment, Olivia lingered and stared at her friend. *I hope you have something here, Kara, otherwise I don't know what we're going to do.*

"I'll be back soon."

Olivia left the car and went inside the apartment building. She went to Kara's apartment and knocked on the door. There was no answer, so she knocked again.

"Just a minute, just a minute. Hold your horses, God damn it."

The Vampire's Omen

Olivia rolled her eyes. After another moment and a lot of shuffling, the door opened, and Magnus Montgomery was standing in front of Olivia.

Magnus, pale-faced with greying hair and holding a cane in one hand, gave Olivia a stern look. "What do you want? Kara ain't here."

Olivia forced a smile. "Hello Mr. Montgomery. I'm here to get something for Kara. May I come in?" she said while motioning towards the door.

Magnus looked confused, but nodded and moved aside so Olivia could enter. "Why didn't she come get it herself?"

"Oh, she's at our friends' place already, and I was on the way so I said I would pick it up for her." Olivia made her way towards Kara's bedroom.

"You're lying," Magnus' stern voice announced.

Olivia turned around and smiled. "Sorry?"

Magnus gave her a stare to rival that of Vasha, and it sent a chill down Olivia's spine. "I used to be a detective, you know. It was my job to tell when people were lying."

Olivia could feel her face flushing, but she knew her vampire complexion would hide it. She kept her smile as best she could. "I don't know what you're talking about, Mr. Montgomery. If you want I can show you the texts."

Magnus snorted. "Yeah, sure you can. Get what you came for and get out," he commanded as he shuffled over to his recliner.

Olivia felt an urge to tell him what was going on, as it was clear he was concerned, but a normal human wouldn't understand. She let out a breath she had been holding in and turned around to go to Kara's bedroom.

Kara's room held a bed, computer, television, and the usual things one would find. Then, littered on the floor, were dirty clothes and papers and flyers. It wasn't as bad as James Moore's place, but it was a stark difference with the rest of the apartment, which Kara no doubt cleaned as Magnus couldn't.

Olivia went straight for Kara's closet, the most likely place she would stash something like human blood. Hanging on the racks there were several different hoodies, sweaters, and long-sleeved shirts in Kara's style. Below the racks, there were piles of jeans and other shirts all in a mess on the floor. Olivia couldn't tell which were dirty and which were clean.

She moved the clothes around and searched for some hidden compartment or cooler that might hold blood, but she couldn't find anything. After a thorough hunt, Olivia moved to the rest of the room. She looked inside DVD cases, books, cabinets and drawers, everywhere she thought one might hide something, and the most she could find was Kara's stash of weed.

Damn it, Kara. Don't you plan ahead?

Olivia let out a sigh and left the room. She made her way towards the door, pensively looking at the floor as she moved forward.

"Whatever's going on," Magnus said over his shoulder, bringing Olivia out of her stupor, "you'd better make sure Kara is safe."

Olivia stared at Magnus, but all she could do was give him a nod. He returned the nod, and then turned back in his chair.

That's right. I have to make sure she's all right. She saved my life, now it's my turn to save hers.

Olivia steeled herself, and left the apartment. She got back into the car in the passenger seat and glanced back at Kara. She was still asleep, but her breathing seemed steady now.

"Did you find anything?"

Olivia shook her head. "No."

Raymond looked downcast. "What will we do then?"

"Do you know if a vampire can suck the blood of another vampire?" Olivia asked, squinting her eyes.

Raymond looked taken aback. "Uhh, I'm not exactly sure. I'm fairly certain the reason why we have to drink blood is because of the nutrients found in it. I don't know the science behind it though, so I could be wrong."

"So our blood doesn't have those nutrients?"

"Not normally, no. When we eat food, our bodies don't get the same nutrients humans do through digestion. That's why we need the blood, because our bodies developed the ability to absorb the nutrients from it instead."

"Damn," Olivia swore, biting her lip.

Raymond pushed up his glasses and fiddled with his hair. "But, I mean, the bloodstream is how those nutrients are transferred throughout our bodies, so it stands to reason that if we have recently fed ourselves, then our bloodstream will then contain those nutrients."

Olivia stared at Raymond. "You think so?"

14

The Vampire's Omen

Raymond shrugged his shoulders. "Maybe."

"I hope this works. Take us somewhere where there aren't any people."

Raymond turned on the car, and proceeded to head to a parking garage.

"I thought you said it's wrong to force the blood of the living down Kara's throat?"

Olivia frowned. "I know, I'm being a little hypocritical, but Kara is against taking blood from living humans. Besides, I'm sure if someone was willing to offer their blood to her she wouldn't refuse."

"Let's hope you're right."

Raymond found a parking garage after a few minutes, and they parked in a secluded location with little traffic. Olivia and Raymond got in the back seat and Raymond cradled Kara's head in his lap.

He opened Kara's mouth, and Olivia pulled up her sleeve. "Ready?" Raymond asked.

"I hope this works." Olivia took out a pocket knife, cleaned it with sanitizing gel and then used a lighter to burn the bacteria away—just in case. Then she cut her arm.

She winced as the blade pushed its way through layers of skin just below her wrist. She cut deep to ensure enough blood would drain, and that meant it would leave a scar, but it would be one she would wear with pride. It would hopefully serve as a reminder of her helping her friend.

The blood dripped from Olivia's arm into Kara's mouth. The red, viscous, life-giving liquid transferred to Kara, and she had no choice but to accept the drink.

Olivia pressed on her arm to push the blood out faster. After what they thought was a decent amount fell into Kara's mouth, Raymond handed Olivia gauze from a first aid kit. Raymond then helped wrap a bandage around Olivia's arm.

"Now we wait," Raymond said.

Olivia and Raymond waited in the back seat of the car with Kara's body lying on top of them. The two switched off taking naps for a few hours. Olivia was leaning against the door of the car, her eyes closed, when a familiar voice met her ears.

"Liv, Ray?"

Olivia opened her eyes and looked over to see her friend waking up as well. "Kara!" she yelled as she moved to hug Kara.

The two hugged while she was still on top of Raymond, and he too joined in as much as possible by leaning forward and wrapping his arms around them both. They laughed at his attempt, and Olivia got back up and sat down.

"So, I guess we won?" Kara said with a weak smile.

Olivia chuckled. "Yeah, we won."

3. RETURN TO THE SCENE OF THE CRIME

"I'm sorry, Kara. If there was any other way, then we would have done it, but we were desperate."

Kara looked away from her friend, thinking on her moral stance, and the question of Olivia's blood being freely offered against it. The leather of the door became her focus, and she could hear her friends shuffling in the front seats.

After a few minutes, Kara let out a sigh. "I guess I never thought of the possibility that someone would offer their blood willingly," she commented.

Olivia's face lit up, but she still seemed wary. "Right? I mean why would it happen? It's probably never happened before," she said, glancing from Kara to Raymond and back.

"I don't blame you, you made your choice. And I guess I don't have a problem with it. I just think I'm going to need some time to let my mind get over it."

Olivia looked like she was about to cry.

"It's alright, Olivia, really. I'm fine with it," Kara said with a smile. "You probably saved my life. Who knows if that doctor was right? He doesn't know anything about psychics."

Olivia nodded and forced a smile.

"Now what do we do?" Raymond asked.

For a moment, the three of them pondered the question in silence. Olivia was the first to speak.

"Well, as I see it we have two choices," she said. "We can run and hide, or we can take the fight to the bastard who attacked us."

"I think we both know which option you want," Kara chuckled. Raymond laughed as well, and Olivia had a devious grin on her face. "So, where should we start if we want to find this assassin, Miss Private Investigator?"

Olivia put her hand up to her chin. "Hmm. I think it would be best to start back at my place, and see if there is anything that he dropped or left behind by accident. If we find anything, I know some of Vasha's contacts who might be able to tell us who it is."

"That sounds as good a place as any. Any other ideas, Raymond?"

"Nothing I can think of," he replied as he started the car.

"Alright, let's go catch this asshole."

Raymond drove them back to Olivia's, and when they entered the apartment the building manager met them in the lobby.

"Olivia, thank God you're safe!" the older gentleman said.

"Thank you for your concern. Luckily we avoided getting injured."

"So you were there when it happened. What exactly did happen, anyway?"

"I'll let you know when I find out, Steven. Has anyone come to my apartment since I left?"

The older man scratched his head. "I'm not sure when you left, but a detective showed up and took a look inside the apartment. He wanted to know where you were, but I didn't know where you went so he left. I offered your phone number but he refused."

The three glanced at each other, and they all wanted to know the same thing. "What was the detective's name?" Olivia asked.

"Detective Simmons. He didn't leave any contact information, so I don't know how you'll contact him."

"Don't worry about it. Could you please hire someone to clean up and repair my apartment? Send the bill to me and I'll have my insurance handle it."

"Sure thing, Olivia." Olivia motioned for the three of them to leave. "Uhh, where are you going?"

She glanced over her shoulder. "I'm going to be staying with some friends until the apartment is repaired. Thanks Steven," she said with a wave.

"You're welcome," he replied.

The three of them exited the apartment building.

"I can't believe Detective Simmons is involved in this again," Kara commented.

"If he's not the person who hired that assassin, then he definitely knows something about it."

The Vampire's Omen

Kara had her brows furrowed. "Why would Simmons be after us again?" she asked.

"Why was he after us in the first place?" Olivia countered.

"Should we find him and question him?" Raymond asked.

"No, we could just be giving him an opportunity to attack us himself if he hired the guy, and he doesn't strike me as the type to give in so easily. We'd just be wasting our time."

Kara raised her brow. "So why can't we search the apartment?"

"We can't go back in there for the time being. Simmons might have bugged it."

"So if we can't search the apartment, what can we do?" Raymond questioned.

"I'm not sure," Olivia answered.

"What about where he shot the bullet from? I saw the direction the bullet came from, and from the angle there's only one building he could have shot from."

Olivia smiled. "You surprise me sometimes, Kara. Lead the way."

Kara beamed from her friend's praise, and took them all to the only building which could reach the height of Olivia's apartment. The roof was just the right height for someone to be able to shoot from. The three of them went to the roof to search for something the assassin might have left behind.

The roof was spacious, easy to access, and the only people who could see onto it were those in Olivia's building. The perimeter of the roof was blocked with a chest-level wall.

"Look at the wall here, it's the perfect level to place a sniper rifle," Olivia commented.

They all went over to the edge of the building on the side where they could see Olivia's apartment from. Kara moved to the position where she thought the assassin might have shot from judging off the height and where she was sitting.

"This looks like where he might have been standing."

"What do you think we should be looking for, Kara?" Olivia asked.

"Well, he shot the bullet, and then he immediately attacked you, right?" The others answered in the affirmative. "And you injured him before he ran away?" They once again answered yes. "Then he didn't have any time to clean up. Maybe the bullet shell is still here."

Olivia and Raymond nodded and smiled, and then the three of them got started searching the area. The roof was littered with the occasional fast food wrapper and beer bottle, no doubt from residents having parties. The cold air of fall circled against the walls of the roof, increasing the wind chill. As they searched, they had to breathe into their hands to warm them up.

"Found it!" Raymond shouted.

Kara and Olivia ran over to see him pointing beside a beer bottle. Right next to it, sitting cradled between the side of the bottle and the roof was a long metal cylinder. Raymond picked up and chucked the bottle to the side, and it broke as it crashed.

Olivia pulled gloves out and put them on before picking up the metal bullet shell. Kara and Raymond both leaned in, pressing their bodies up against Olivia, as she examined the shell. All along the sides of the shell there was an etched pattern that looked like a Celtic design.

"This design must have been etched by the assassin. Bullets don't come like this," Olivia said as she laughed.

"At least non-decorative ones," Kara added.

"So, the contact you know should be able to identify this?" Raymond asked.

"I think so. Vasha trusts him with finding people she can't, so I imagine if he can't tell us, we won't know anyone else to turn to."

"Let's get going. We don't know if the assassin is still after us or not."

The three left the building, bullet casing in hand, and headed to Olivia's contact.

Olivia guided Raymond to a remote pawn shop called Honest Herman's. It was located across from a small strip mall and a used car dealership, all of which didn't seem to see much traffic, foot or otherwise. The shops and cars all seemed older than all three of them, and in need of some cleaning. The pawn shop in particular had an old sign with lights missing, and a front window showing some dust-covered wares.

When they entered the establishment, a bell tinged against the door and announced their presence. They received no greeting, however, and no one seemed to be manning the register.

The pawn shop itself was lined with shelves filled to the brim with a multitude of different items. On one side there were various musical instruments including guitars and drums and the like, and on another wall there were masks and other artifacts that could have been fakes, but gave the feel of being authentic. The centre of the store was similar in its random assortment of things for sale, from the strange, almost occult-looking, to new electronics.

Kara felt something ancient within the walls of the store, unlike anything she had felt before. It was strange, but neither good nor evil. She pushed the thought out of her mind. *Sometimes I hate these powers,* she thought.

Olivia went up to the counter and struck a bell on it. The sound resonated throughout the shop, but no one answered its call. She kept dinging the bell for ten seconds straight before someone yelled "I'm coming, I'm coming," from the back.

Before long, a diminutive, pale man walked out from an open door to the back, and when he noticed Olivia and the others his eyes lit up. "Olivia! Aren't you a sight for sore eyes," he said as he rushed over to her.

Olivia knelt down and the two hugged for a moment. "It's nice to see you as well, Herman," she replied.

Herman pulled away, then went to the counter and sat on a stool. "What brings you to Honest Herman's?"

"We're wondering if you can help us find out who this belongs to," she said as she pulled out the bullet shell and placed it upright on the counter.

Herman peered at the shell for a moment with wrinkled brows before he pulled out some spectacles from his breast pocket and put them on. Herman leaned over the counter, moving to the left and the right as he examined the shell. After a moment, all the while muttering "hmms" and "haahs," he picked up the casing and inspected it further.

After a few minutes he looked up at Olivia, Kara, and Raymond, and began slapping the casing against the palm of his hand. "You sure you want to know about this?"

"How do you think we got that? We have no choice."

Herman smirked. "I don't know who you pissed off, but it must have been someone important. This is from a hitman called the Celtic Butcher. He's former Irish Special Forces, and a powerful psychic. If he's after you, you've got your work cut out for you."

"We managed to fend him off in his first attack, but just barely. That's why we want to take the fight to him."

Herman's eyes widened and he leaned back in his stool. "That's impressive. How did you manage that?" Olivia and Raymond both looked at Kara. Herman adjusted his spectacles. "Ah, yes, I understand. You had your own psychic assistance. I see."

Kara looked away, expecting an attack that never came.

"So, you want to attack him before he comes at you again?"

"That's right. Do you know how to find him?"

Herman nodded. "I'll need to call in a favour from someone, but I can get you his address. I'll be back in a moment." Herman got down from his stool and went into the back of the shop.

The three of them all glanced at each other with confident smiles on their faces. Soon they would have what they needed, and their final showdown with the Celtic Butcher would begin.

4. SENSE OF GUILT

Address in hand, Olivia, Kara, and Raymond left Honest Herman's.

"Now that we have the address, we have to come up with a plan," Kara suggested.

"I think we need to see his place before we can come up with anything. It's better if we have an idea of what his house looks like, and then we can plan how to enter and where to strike," Olivia commented.

Raymond looked at the address written down on a piece of paper in Olivia's hand. "The address isn't far. Let's go now, and then we can plan."

The three of them entered Raymond's car and headed to the address. The Celtic Butcher lived in a middle class urban neighbourhood, which surprised them all. From what they could see, the houses were populated mainly by families, all of whom had children. Some parents were out in their yards playing with their kids on swing sets and with other toys.

They pulled up in front of the house, and were not surprised to see that it looked like all the others along the street. The assassin's house was two storeys of a drab white color with curtains blocking all the windows.

"This is it," Raymond said.

"Do you sense anything, Kara?"

Kara focussed her mind on the house, but she couldn't feel any psychic energy in the vicinity. "No, I don't think he's in there."

Olivia frowned. "It's a chance we'll have to take. If he's not here, this is the perfect time to bust in and set a trap. We'll attack him when he returns home, when he least expects it."

Kara leaned forward in the back seat, concern evident on her face. "What if there are other people in the house? I can only sense psychics, I can't sense anyone else. He could have a family."

Olivia glanced at Kara and then Raymond, who had the same concern written on his face. "If there's someone else in there, then we'll deal with them." Olivia went for the door handle, to leave and put an end to any arguments, but Kara stopped her.

Kara felt something stir inside her, like a twinge of guilt and sadness that awaited them if they entered that home. "Olivia, I'm getting a bad feeling. We shouldn't be doing this."

"Did you have a vision of us dying?"

"No, nothing like that. I'm just getting a bad feeling that if we enter that house we're going to regret it."

"If we don't die, how can we regret it?" Olivia argued.

Kara was a loss for words. She didn't know how to express what she wanted to say, and so Olivia shrugged and left the car. Raymond wore a sad smile as he looked at Kara, and then he too exited the car. Kara followed soon after, pushing the feeling out of her mind.

The three of them crossed the street to the house. Olivia used her honed vampiric senses to scan the area. After a moment of watching and walking towards the home, she motioned for the others to follow her, and they ran to the side of the house.

Along the side of the house, at the bottom, there was a window to access the basement. They all glanced around, checking to see if anyone was looking their way, or if the neighbours were looking out their windows. Kara used her powers to move the neighbours' curtains out of the way just to be doubly sure no one was watching.

Olivia kicked in the window and used her foot to clear the glass shards out of the way. Then she knelt down and moved a black curtain out of the way. Raymond entered the basement first, followed by Kara.

Kara fell to her knees on the concrete floor of the Celtic Butcher's basement. When she rose to her feet she peered around, and what she saw confirmed that they were in the correct home.

In the little light afforded by the window they entered through, Kara could see tables filled with weapons of all kinds: swords, knives, guns—both automatic and manual—and the tools to care for them.

The Vampire's Omen

On one end of the basement, there looked to be a training area with wrestling mats, a martial arts dummy, and a target for throwing knives. There was also other miscellaneous equipment that Kara didn't recognize, but it looked high tech and new. On one of the tables, she could see a drill station, and bullets lying around it.

Olivia jumped into the basement behind Kara, and when she got to her feet she whistled. "This is our guy, no question."

Kara went over to one of the tables filled with guns, and when she looked at them she felt the same feeling of guilt she'd felt since they approached the house. As Olivia made her way to the stairs to the main floor, Kara looked around. Her eyes fell on a plaque in the centre of the room.

"'For one, many,'" she read. *What does that mean?*

There was a loud snap at the top of the steps, then the creaking of a door. "The lights are off, looks like no one's home," Olivia whispered. "C'mon, let's go."

Kara walked backwards a few steps, staring at the plaque for another moment before she turned around and went up the steps with Raymond.

The basement stairs brought them into the kitchen of the main level, which had a completely different feel than the basement.

The kitchen was spotless, and had all the best amenities for someone who seemed to love cooking, including nice, well-worn equipment. The dining room was right next to the kitchen. There was a large wooden table for several people to sit at, and it had a nice white table cloth and a cornucopia centerpiece. Above the table was a crystal chandelier with candles and light bulbs.

The three of them went from the dining room to the entrance— where a flight of stairs led to the second floor—over to a living room. The living room had a nice large couch and a television above a fireplace, as well as a computer in the corner.

"Tch. This guy must be making bank off the lives he takes," Olivia commented.

Kara went over to the unlit fireplace, and looked at some framed pictures over a mantle. She picked up one picture and turned it to the outside light to get a better look. In the frame was an older gentleman with a strong jaw and toned muscles kneeling next to a child in a

Shawn Wiseman

wheelchair. They were both smiling, and they looked like they had just been playing catch with a baseball.

Kara placed the picture down and clutched the mantle. She closed her eyes and tried to push away what she saw. *This man is going to kill us if we don't kill him,* she tried repeating in her mind over and over.

"What's wrong, Kara?" Raymond asked.

Kara handed him the picture. Raymond looked at it for a moment before placing it back on the mantle shelf. He turned Kara around and made her face him. "Kara, we can handle this on our own. You can leave us here," he said.

Kara shied away from Raymond's gaze. She was torn between both options, because of the possibilities of both. If she stayed, she would have to kill the Butcher, and that meant all the possible consequences that came with it. If she left, the Butcher could kill Raymond and Olivia. And, for some reason, perhaps because of the overwhelming guilt she was feeling, the Butcher's death felt like the worse option.

"What?" Olivia questioned.

"I don't think Kara can do what's necessary."

Olivia looked confused, and then saw Kara's face. Raymond handed her the picture. Olivia took a look at it for a few seconds before throwing it to the ground. The frame and glass shattered on contact.

"This is horseshit, Kara! You're having second thoughts just because he might have a crippled kid?" she shouted. "He almost killed us, and if he finishes us off, he'll go on to kill other people."

Kara was on the verge of tears. "I just don't know what's right in this situation. All this guilt I feel in this place is messing with my mind. I know all that you're saying, but I just don't think killing him is the right thing to do."

Olivia let out an angry sigh. "We don't have time for this," she said. She looked at Raymond. "We need to plan how we're going to attack. Kara, if you're going to join us, do it soon, otherwise you might get caught in the middle."

Olivia's verbal slap in the face had the intended effect, but it was the wrong timing.

26

The Vampire's Omen

The door of the home flung open, sending a cold wind in through the frame. A man jumped inside holding a gun. He took aim at the three vampires and pulled the trigger.

Kara was still reeling from the guilt and Olivia's version of a pep talk, and her reaction time was dulled. She couldn't make a decision on whether she should attempt using telekinesis again, or to move out of the way.

Raymond jumped to the side out of the way, and Olivia was about to follow until she noticed Kara looking like a deer caught in headlights. Olivia jumped in front of Kara and pulled her out of the way, but she took a bullet in her side, and fell to the ground.

"Liv!" Kara shouted.

Olivia clutched her side as blood seeped out of it. "I'm fine. It only grazed me," she said through winces.

"I tell ye I was quite surprised ta see yer car parked outside," a voice with an Irish accent came from somewhere in the house. "Ye did a number on me side there, missy. Glad I could return the favour."

Raymond got up and started to leave Kara and Olivia.

"Raymond, no! We have to stay together!" Kara whispered, but he didn't listen. He went off deeper into the house.

Olivia tied her jacket tight around her waist and then she moved forward in a crouched position towards the back of the house. She inched her way forward, listening for any sound within the house. Kara mimicked her, but she wasn't able to hear anything. It was beyond quiet. Too quiet if a normal human was moving through the house. Even ex-special forces would be no match for a vampire's ears, and yet nothing.

The plaster of the wall next to Kara exploded as a fist rammed through it and hit her on the side of the head. Kara fell to the ground on her shoulder, and her arm popped out of place with a loud crack. She screamed out in pain. Olivia rushed to her aid. The Celtic Butcher moved into the living room.

Olivia turned around and gritted her teeth, then bared her fang. She jumped towards him with a snarl, her fang and claws poised to strike. The Butcher moved his hand down towards the floor, and used his powers to force Olivia to the floor as well. She was on her knees, and fighting against the psychic power. She made eye contact with him.

"Kara!" Olivia screamed. "Use your powers! I'm trying to restrain his."

Kara turned around and sat up as best she could. She looked at the corner of Olivia's eyes, and could see something akin to Vasha's psychic-numbing eyes, but it wasn't as powerful. She pushed away the pain in her shoulder and focussed on the man in front of her. She thrust out her good hand and set her fist into a ball.

The man's eyes went wide, and he ran away without a sound. He disappeared into the house once again.

Olivia was able to move again, and she started to run after him. "No, Olivia!" Kara said, pushing herself up to her feet. Olivia stopped in her tracks. "We need to stay together."

"Thas right, you have a psychic with ye. Never thought I'd see the day when a psychic teamed up with a bloody vampire," the man shouted.

"Can you fix my arm?" Kara asked.

Olivia grabbed Kara's arm and gave it a swift tug. With another pop, Kara's arm was back in place. She bit her lip and suppressed another scream. She moved her arm around, but it still hurt too much to use. She motioned to Olivia that she was alright, and the two of them followed after the Butcher.

They went through the house, peering around every corner, until they made their way back to the other side of the kitchen. They could hear noise. Footsteps approached. Olivia tensed and looked at Kara. Kara concentrated her mind, and nodded.

Olivia and Kara both jumped into the kitchen. Kara used her powers to lift the man into the air, and Olivia went to strike, but stopped short. They'd almost attacked Raymond.

Kara let Raymond down to the ground. "Where is he?" she asked.

Raymond shrugged his shoulders. "I checked upstairs then came back down when I heard the commotion. I heard his voice coming from this direction, so I came this way."

Where did he go? Kara pondered the question for a few seconds, and then it dawned on her and the others at the same time.

The Vampire's Omen

They all looked at the entrance to the basement, and then rushed to go down before the Butcher could claim his arsenal. When they looked down into the shadows, they saw the barrel of a gun staring up at them from the bottom of the stairs.

Bullets from an automatic weapon sped towards them. Kara didn't hesitate this time, and used her powers to push them all out of the way. Bullets cascaded through the wood of the house and sent chips bounding around the kitchen. The bullets hit the windows in the kitchen and glass joined the wood. Kara helped her friends into the dining room, and then let them go on the floor.

The three of them continued running to the entrance, and then up the stairs to the second floor. When they reached the top of the steps, Olivia and Kara went right. Kara glanced over her shoulder to see Raymond heading the opposite direction, but bullets hot on their heels shunted any thought of going back for him out of her head.

Olivia pulled Kara into one of the rooms, and they took cover behind a bed. Kara glanced over the edge of the bed at the door. She used her powers to close it silently. "If he enters, I'll use my powers to bind him, and you use your eye to suppress his powers," Kara whispered.

"I don't know if I'll be able to hold him for long. Vasha didn't teach me. I'm just going off of what you told me."

"It'll have to do," Kara replied. *No teacher and yet you still learned how to do that? Just what kind of training are you doing, Liv?*

The room they were in looked like a boy's room, with posters and toys and colourful sheets on the bed. There were also some pictures hung on the wall, with the boy and the Butcher playing together like the one on the mantle downstairs. There was no mistaking that he must be the father.

Footsteps approached. Olivia and Kara tensed and held their breath. There was a loud snap and a crash as the Butcher busted down one of the other doors. More footsteps came to their door. After a second, the door flew open, and the Butcher raised his gun.

Kara put a barrier on the trigger, locking it in place. That gave her and Olivia just enough time to stand up. Olivia focused her gaze on him, and he seemed to be in a light stupor, but it was only on the surface. Kara bound his entire body with her powers, stopping his movement. When he pushed back against the fog in his mind, she could feel him testing the barrier. He was stronger than her, even with Olivia working her magic.

Olivia was sweating from the effort. Whatever that ability was, it was taking a toll on her. "I can't move. You need to kill him, Kara."

Kara was holding her hand out, rapt in the force she was exerting on the Butcher. She shook her head. "We don't have to," she replied. Before Olivia could object, Kara talked again. She stared straight at the Butcher. "It doesn't have to end like this. We don't know who called on you to kill us, but if you just let it go we can all walk away from this alive."

Sweat beaded on the Butcher's forehead, and his lips curled into a smile. "That ain't how it works, missy," he replied. "You look like a smart lass, you should already know how this has to end."

The tension in the room was thick. The power pulsating in the room made the air dense and hard to breathe. The smoke that was their psychic powers was choking their minds and bodies, sucking the energy out of them.

Kara clenched her teeth as she held the binding firm. "We don't… You have a son, don't you?" she asked. "What's going to happen without you there for him?"

"Ain't ye just the sweetest? You never killed a'fore, have ye? Ye best blacken yer soul quick-like. The world we live in ain't the place for tender hearts," the Butcher warned.

Tears streamed down Kara's face. "Please," she begged. "Please don't make me do this."

Before the Butcher could answer, a hand burst through his stomach. The force of the blow lifted the Butcher into the air. He looked over his shoulder to behold his killer before he coughed up blood and his eyes went listless. The killer removed their hand, and the Butcher fell to the ground.

Kara mimicked the fall and her knees hit the carpeted floor with an equal thud. The Butcher was bleeding out, and was going to die. There was nothing she could do to save him now.

She felt weak and sick. She looked over to see Raymond at the entrance to the room, his hand covered in blood up to his forearm, and he was looking at her with concern written on his face.

The Vampire's Omen

Kara wept noiselessly on the floor of the room as she stared at the man's face. All joy the others felt from their victory over the assassin was lost in the ether by Kara's tears. Olivia hugged her friend as she cried.

Kara's thoughts went in all different directions, most of them questions about the boy in the photograph, and just why the boy's father was an assassin. Her thoughts eventually came back to the feeling she'd had before entering the house, and she questioned the source of the guilt she felt.

The sound of sirens hit their sensitive vampire ears. Olivia glanced over her shoulder towards the front of the house. "We need to leave," she said.

Kara nodded and wiped her eyes. With Olivia's help she got up and then the three of them went downstairs. They walked through the dining room and the kitchen, past the open basement and out a door at the back of the house.

As Olivia checked for anyone watching, Raymond cleaned his arm of blood. After telling the others it was clear, they left the house and circled their way around the other houses. After putting some distance between them and the assassin's house, they went back to the street and walked casually back to their car as police cars began pulling up.

The police noticed them approach, and after a preliminary question about why they'd parked there, and Olivia saying they were in a nearby park—and an added touch of asking what was going on—the police let them go. Olivia sat with Kara in the back and held her hand.

Raymond drove them away from the house. "I took this off the Butcher," he said while holding up a phone. "I thought we could use it to see who hired him."

Olivia took the phone and began looking through it. There was no lock on it, it seemed.

Kara let out a sigh and let go of Olivia's hand. "I think I'm better now," she said. "I just think it was that house. Something about it... There was so much guilt I could feel when entering it."

Olivia glanced over at her friend. "Do you think it was another of your powers? Was it his emotions you were feeling?"

Kara shook her head. "I'm not sure. It could have been that, or a premonition," she speculated.

Olivia went back to the phone and looked through the text messages. After a moment she blurted out, "Aha!" She showed Kara the phone. "It was Simmons who hired him, see?" She handed the phone to Kara. "He was pretty pissed that Simmons didn't mention anything about you, Kara."

Kara took the phone and looked at the text messages. It showed a clear picture of coded speak about a "job" and Simmons giving him Olivia's address and photo. "It looks like you were the main target, but why? Why is Simmons after you?"

Olivia bit her thumb as she stared out the car window. "I have no idea. I never met the guy before the police brought me in that first time. Maybe he was pissed because I got away?"

"That would make sense if Kara was the target as well, because she attacked him. Whatever the case, there's more questions to this than we have the capacity to answer."

Kara scrolled through the other messages on the phone, and noticed a thread with another person named Jeffery. Guilt pulsing from the phone drew her to the messages. She read them.

> "Hey, how's my big strong lad doing? You coming to see me this weekend?"

"Can't. I'm in the hospital again."

> "Aww. Well, I'll come visit you. A few more jobs and I'll have the money to pay for your operations, and soon enough you won't have to visit there ever again. How's that sound?"

"That would be nice."

> "Lol. What say I get you some fast food to make you feel better?"

The Vampire's Omen

"Yay! Watch out though, Mom's here."

"Keep it our secret and I'll sneak it in for you."

"She won't notice a thing ☺"

"See you soon. Stay strong. Love you."

"Love you too, Dad."

The guilt she felt overwhelmed her again and Kara could think of nothing other than how that boy wasn't going to see his father ever again.

Kara finally understood what the "For one, many" plaque on the Celtic Butcher's basement wall meant. His son was the one, and the people he killed for him were the many. How could she blame the man for doing what he thought he needed to do to save the one he loved?

Tears streamed down her face from remorse over the man they'd killed and the boy who might never know why. As Olivia held her, she kept asking herself if there was any other way it could have gone, but she realised that she would never know the answer.

THE END

THE VAMPIRE'S VICTIM

Book 4 of Shawn Wiseman's debut series

PSYCHICS VS. VAMPIRES

Is on sale now through Amazon, Print and Digital.

ABOUT THE AUTHOR

Shawn Wiseman credits his love of reading and writing to his parents, who taught him how to read from an early age, and fostered his creativity.

After almost becoming a boring businessman, Shawn decided to try his hand at writing, and found his passion. He likes strong characters, lots of action, and punchy dialogue. Some of his vices include video games, swearing like a sailor, and fast food.

Shawn gets inspiration from his friends and family who continue to encourage him with his writing. Before trying his hand at self-publishing, a friend was the one who convinced him to try a writing challenge, and he hasn't looked back since then. His biggest goal is to create characters and stories that will inspire others to try their hand at writing, just as he was inspired before.

It would help Shawn out if you shared this novel with your friends or leave a review on Amazon.